J

THE
KNIGHT'S
ENEMIES

WARRIOR HEROES

Crabtree Publishing Company

www.crabtreebooks.com
1-800-387-7650

616 Welland Ave.
St. Catharines, ON
L2M 5V6

PMB 59051, 350 Fifth Ave.
59th Floor,
New York, NY

Published by Crabtree Publishing Company in 2015.

Author: Benjamin Hulme-Cross

Illustrator: Angelo Rinaldi

Project coordinator: Kelly Spence

Editors: Alex Van Tol, Kathy Middleton

Proofreader: Wendy Scavuzzo

Prepress technician: Tammy McGarr

Print coordinator: Katherine Berti

Copyright © 2014 A & C Black

Text copyright © 2014 Benjamin Hulme-Cross

Illustration copyright © Angelo Rinaldi

Additional illustrations © Shutterstock

First published 2014 by A & C Black, an imprint of Bloomsbury Publishing Plc.

Printed in Canada/022015/IH20141209

Library and Archives Canada Cataloguing in Publication

Hulme-Cross, Benjamin, author
    The knight's enemies / written by Benjamin Hulme-Cross
; illustrated by Angelo Rinaldi.

(Warrior heroes)
First published 2014 by A & C Black.
ISBN 978-0-7787-1765-2 (bound).--
ISBN 978-0-7787-1769-0 (pbk.)

    I. Rinaldi, Angelo, illustrator II. Title.

PZ7.H87397Kn 2015   j823'.92
C2014-907825-0

Library of Congress Cataloging-in-Publication Data

CIP available at the Library of Congress

THE KNIGHT'S ENEMIES

WARRIOR HEROES

BENJAMIN HULME-CROSS

Illustrated by

Angelo Rinaldi

Crabtree Publishing Company

www.crabtreebooks.com

CONTENTS

INTRODUCTION
THE HALL OF HEROES

The Hall of Heroes is a museum
all about warriors throughout
history. It's full of swords, bows
and arrows, helmets, boats, armor,
shields, spears, axes, and just
about anything else that a warrior
might need. But this isn't just
another museum full of old stuff
in glass cases. It's also haunted
by the ghosts of the warriors whose
belongings are kept there.

Our great-grandfather, Professor
Blade, started the museum. When he
died, his ghost began to haunt the
place, too. He felt guilty about the
trapped ghost warriors and vowed
he would not rest in peace until
all the other ghosts were laid to
rest first. And that's where Arthur
and I come in...

On the night of our great-grandfather's funeral, Arthur and I broke into the museum, for old times' sake. We knew it was wrong, but we just couldn't help ourselves. And that's when we discovered something very weird. When one of the ghost warriors touches either one of us, we get transported back to the time and place where that ghost lived and died. And we can't get back until we've fixed whatever it is that keeps the ghost from resting in peace. So Arthur and I go from one mission to the next, recovering lost swords, avenging deaths, saving loved ones, and doing whatever else these ghost warriors need us to do.

Fortunately, while the Professor

was alive, I wrote down everything he ever told us about these warriors in a book I call *Warrior Heroes*. So we do have some idea of what we're getting into each time, even if Arthur does still call me "Finn the geek." But we need more than just a book to survive each adventure, because wherever we go, we're surrounded by war and battle and the fiercest fighters who ever lived--as you're about to find out!

CHAPTER 1

The Professor ushered the boys into his office with a hushed command. "Hurry boys, it won't be long until he arrives." He had just announced that the next warrior to ask for their help would be a medieval knight.

"A quest!" Arthur's eyes gleamed as the door closed behind them. "Now that sounds like a *real* adventure!"

Finn snorted. "Quest! You can forget all that King Arthur stuff."

Arthur rolled his eyes at his brother's attitude.

But the Professor nodded. "Finn's right. They didn't really go in for quests in the way that the stories suggest."

The boys were sitting around their great-grandfather's desk in his study at the museum. A single desk lamp cast little light around the rest of the room.

Finn leaned forward. "Who is this knight, then?" he asked. A clock sitting on the mantel ticked and whirred.

"I'm afraid we don't really know much about him, my boy," the Professor replied. "He lived in England. I think it was during the fifth or sixth century. But that's about all the information we have, so we'll just have to ask him when he gets here. He'll be along soon enough."

"Well, what did knights get up to then?" Arthur inquired. "Jousting? Rescuing damsels? Fighting for the king?"

"Fighting against the king, more like," said Finn. Arthur scowled as his brother corrected him yet again. "There were civil wars and rebellions," Finn continued. "Every time a king died, a whole bunch of people would claim the right to be the next king. Whoever won the argument spent the rest of his or her life trying to fight off challengers."

The Professor smiled. "He's right again, Arthur. Jousting tournaments did happen, but the knight's main job was to fight for his lord whenever he needed him. Knights didn't really fight for the king as such, unless that was what their lord told them to do."

"Fine, whatever," Arthur snapped. Then his face brightened. "I wonder if we'll get to wear armor and ride horses!"

"I hate to disappoint you," the Professor said. Arthur sighed and began tapping a foot impatiently. "Most knights would have worn chain mail at that time rather than armor plates. And a lot of the fighting revolved around laying siege to castles or defending them. You didn't need horses much for that, although you did need a horse to be a knight."

"So they were basically soldiers, then?"

"Exactly," the Professor agreed. "They were well-trained soldiers who could fight on horseback in battle or alongside peasants in castle sieges. They were officers in small armies..."

"Shh!" Finn broke in. "I think I heard something."

They listened intently. The clock had stopped ticking. The only sound breaking the silence was a steady clink as somebody approached the door of the study!

The air in the room grew colder. The lamp flickered and cut out, plunging the room into darkness. Even though Arthur and Finn knew the routine, it made their muscles tingle every time it happened. The door creaked open and closed.

Nobody dared move for a minute. Then, carefully, the Professor lit a candle. Its thin, flickering light faintly illuminated the figure of a knight. His scarred face was smeared with blood that seeped down from under his hood made of chain mail. As he cast his stare around the room, the expression on his face was one of pure anguish.

The boys both stood frozen to the spot, hardly daring to breathe. The Professor cleared his throat. "How can my boys help you, old chap?"

The knight's gaze shifted slowly from one boy to the other. "Eleanor..." he said softly, breathing the word out like a sigh.

"Who was..." Finn faltered. "Who is she?"

"Eleanor," the bloodied knight sighed again. His head slumped forward and his shoulders heaved. "My daughter."

"My dear man," said the Professor, clearing his throat again. "What happened to her?"

"Wroxley Castle was under siege," the knight

began. "It was John the Withered who attacked us. A cruel man. A very cruel man."

"And is that how you died?" The Professor asked. "What is your name?"

"Sir William Mallory," said the knight, looking at the Professor for the first time. "Yes, yes, I died in the siege at the hands of a traitor."

"And Eleanor?"

"They took her. A spy kidnapped her during the siege. My only child," the knight groaned. "And her mother long since dead."

"Then your daughter lived?" Arthur prompted.

The knight shook his head slightly in his chain mail hood.

"Not content to be feared by the peasants, John the Withered wanted *the lords* to fear him, too." Sir William broke off and put his hands to his head. "They sent Eleanor's head back to me the following morning..." he trailed off, seeming to gasp for air.

Finn stole a glance at his brother, whose horrified expression mirrored his own. Cautiously, he said, "Then you want us to–"

"Save her!" Sir William cried. "Save her! Save her in any way you can!" Sir William lurched forward toward the boys, hands outstretched.

"Wait! You need to tell us more!" Arthur shouted, but it was too late. A ghostly hand gripped each boy by the neck. The air filled with mist so thick that nothing of the room could be seen. The candle flickered and died, and the boys saw only darkness.

CHAPTER 2

Arthur became aware of a steady, far-off roar, like the sea heard from a distance. His mind reached out toward the sound and it grew louder. He blinked his eyes against the darkness, but he could still see nothing. Gradually, he began to make out more sounds intermingled with the roar. He realized they were shouts, though they still sounded distant.

Where am I? he wondered, noticing for the first time how cold he was. The air around him began to move, and he had the strange sensation that he was falling backward.

Shadowy figures appeared in front of a shimmering light before him. It was only as his mouth filled with icy water that he realized he was looking up at the sky. *I'm underwater,* he thought calmly. Then he awoke. Suddenly terrified, he thrashed around in the water. His foot struck something hard, and he kicked up toward daylight.

Chest burning, he shot up through the water. He broke the surface, gulping in a huge, spluttering lungful of air. He twisted around to the sound of shouting and saw that he was in a fast-flowing river. A steep, rocky bank was slipping quickly by in a blur of green.

"Quick, boy!" someone yelled.

The water spun Arthur around as it whisked him along. To his horror, he saw that he was fast approaching a watermill. Its giant paddles churned slowly through water that swirled and bubbled ominously.

He kicked and thrashed toward the bank, and his hand brushed against a stone. It was worn smooth by the river and he slid helplessly on.

"Help!" Arthur cried, swallowing mouthfuls of icy water. The paddles churned closer and closer.

"Here, boy! You only have one chance." A man sprinting along the bank next to Arthur soon pulled ahead and stood in between him and the mill. The man reached down and held a long staff over the water. Arthur bobbed toward the staff, twisting desperately to position himself. A moment later, he had it in both hands. His head dipped below the water as the current tugged him around. One hand slipped off the staff, and he felt the other beginning to slide. As the creak of the mill got louder, Arthur closed his eyes.

I wonder whether Finn is doing any better, he thought. The relentless current sucked him onward.

Then strong hands gripped him by the wrists. They dragged him quickly out of the water, scraping his chest painfully over stones before rolling him onto his back. He lay there coughing water out of his lungs and blinking up at his rescuer. A big man with curly, brown hair and a thick beard stared down at him.

Arthur sat up, still coughing. "Where am I?" he spluttered.

"Where are you? The water must have washed away your wits. You are outside Wroxley Castle." The man nodded his head in the direction of a large stone wall that rose up from the top of the riverbank.

"Oh yes," Arthur said. "Wroxley. I remember. Uh... Thank you sir."

"You may have the chance to repay me sooner than you think," the man replied. "Men loyal to John the Withered are advancing on the castle as we speak, laying waste to the villages. People from miles hence are fleeing to the castle gates and begging to be admitted. I am one of them. Perchance you can persuade the guards to let me in."

"I hate to disappoint you," said Arthur, thinking quickly. "But they don't know me at the castle either."

The man's face fell, and he began walking briskly away. Clearly he had no more use for Arthur.

"Wait!" Arthur shouted. "Do you have a name? I'll tell them you saved me."

"I am Adam," the man replied over his shoulder without stopping. "We must get to the gatehouse. Soon they will close the gates."

* * * * *

Finn felt as though he was rattling around in a barrel with a brick. His head banged repeatedly against something hard, and his body was being shaken and bumped from all directions. He opened his eyes to the weak gray light that seeped through a forest canopy overhead. Something pressed hard on his leg, and he looked down to see a pig rolling onto his foot. *I must be in some sort of cart*, he thought.

He pulled his leg back and tried to stand up. He slipped and staggered backward until his legs hit a low barrier. He toppled sideways out of the cart. He cursed as he landed hard on a muddy path.

A thin line of ragged, dejected-looking people were making their hurried way along the forest track. Many of them were wailing and groaning. A couple of people glanced briefly at the strange boy who had suddenly appeared, but nobody stopped or spoke to him as they rushed past. Finn dusted himself off where he sat and waited for the miserable procession to pass, and tried to remember where he was.

For a few minutes, everything was a blank. It always took a while to remember the details after shifting in time. Finn's mind gradually cleared and he remembered Sir William. *Save his daughter Eleanor–that's the mission. But what does she need saving from?* His thoughts were interrupted by the steady beat of a horse's hooves.

A teenage boy on horseback galloped round a bend in the track. He slowed his mount to a canter as he approached Finn through the trees.

"Quick, boy," the rider shouted, reining the horse in. "John the Withered and his men are a mile hence and advancing. They have laid waste to everything in their path, and they are showing mercy to none. To Wroxley Castle if you value your life!"

Finn got to his feet warily.

"Which way?" he asked.

"Which way?" The young man looked at Finn as if he were an idiot. "Come," he said, reaching down. "Climb up. I am Thomas Shipton, squire. Your name?"

"Finn Blade, traveler," he said, reaching out to grab hold of the friendly outstretched hand. As he did, he noticed a movement in the forest behind Thomas.

"Look out!" he shouted. Instinctively, Thomas hunched down into the horse's mane. An arrow hissed between the two boys and thudded into a tree.

The squire threw a panicked glance over his shoulder before turning back to Finn. "Climb up," he said urgently, holding out a slightly shakier hand this time. Finn grabbed it and swung himself up onto the horse behind Thomas just in time to avoid a second arrow that flew past at head height. Thomas kicked the horse's sides to speed them away, but as he did, the horse reared up, neighing. Finn slid backward and landed hard in the mud for the second time that day. Thomas shouted in alarm as his horse staggered sideways on its hind legs, then toppled heavily to the ground. An arrow protruded from its flank. Finn felt the ground shake as the horse landed, pinning Thomas's foot to the ground.

The archers gave a triumphant shout, and Finn looked up to see two men roaring and running forward. He crawled behind the horse and lay next to Thomas, who was trying to free his foot from the heavy weight of the animal. The bow Thomas had slung across his back bounced in

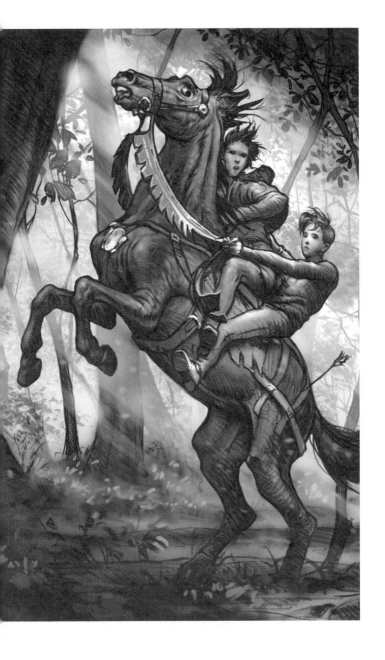

the air as he tried to kick himself free. Finn grabbed it and wrestled it up over Thomas's head.

"Arrows?" Finn asked, breathlessly. Thomas pushed himself up on one elbow, revealing a quiver that had been trapped beneath him. Finn slipped the strap of the quiver over Thomas's head and snatched out an arrow, notching it to the bowstring with fluent ease. If he had to fight, then archery was his thing. Taking a deep breath, he pushed himself up on one knee and took aim at one of the archers. They were seconds away now, sprinting toward him. But their eyes widened when they saw the danger they were in. Finn drew the string back, took aim at the larger of the two men, and released. The man collapsed to the ground, gurgling horribly as he clutched at the arrow lodged in his throat. His companion stopped abruptly and raised his bow. Both he and Finn reached for arrows at the same moment. Time seemed to slow down. The two adversaries knew that life and death depended on being the first to shoot. In almost perfect unison, they notched arrows and took aim. *Too close to call*, thought Finn. As he let his arrow fly, he ducked his head back down behind the horse. He heard both arrows whistle through the air. Then Finn felt the horse shudder slightly. At the same time, the other archer cried out in pain.

Finn notched another arrow and sprang sideways out from behind the horse. He could see now that a third arrow wouldn't be necessary. His enemy lay motionless on his back, an arrow buried deep in his chest.

Finn sank back to the ground, his heart

hammering. For a few moments, there was complete silence. Then Thomas began calling out. "Finn? Are you hit? Finn?"

Finn crawled back around the horse to Thomas's side.

"Both dead," he panted.

"Then I owe you my life," said Thomas, wincing in pain. "But we must be gone or else we will be killed before I can repay the debt." He tried again to pull his foot out from beneath the horse before slumping down and looking up at Finn desperately. Suddenly the horse whimpered and arched its back. The weight shifted and Thomas yanked his foot free. It was the horse's final act.

"Is she alive?" Thomas whispered. Finn looked down at the motionless animal and saw that a second arrow was lodged in her chest. He shook his head, and Thomas's face grew pale.

"Come on," said Finn kindly. "I'll help you to the castle. Can you walk?"

"My ankle is bruised, that is all. I can walk."

Thomas and Finn set off along the track, glancing nervously over their shoulders from time to time. They finally emerged from the forest, and Finn caught his first sight of Wroxley Castle. He studied it hard, trying to take in and memorize every detail that could possibly be of use later.

The castle was simple, but forbidding. Topped with battlements, the outer wall formed a square, each side of which looked to be around 160 feet (50 meters) long. To Finn, it seemed almost like the eastern side of the outer wall rose up out of the river. The river would act as a natural defense against attack from that direction. He could also see a moat, which was fed by the river, likely bordered the other three sides of the castle. On the western side, away from the river, a large, square gatehouse was visible, thrusting up and out from the outer wall, protecting the entrance. Finn could not see clearly, but he knew from his conversations with the Professor that the drawbridge would provide access across the moat and through the gatehouse. Men defending the castle's entrance were protected inside the gatehouse as they rained down arrows and stones on attackers.

The main castle building, called the keep, was a huge, dark, cube of stone. Finn could see the four short towers jutting up from the top corners. But the building was strangely situated. Usually, the keep sat in the center of the square created by the outer wall, but this was not the case here. The keep stood right up against the eastern side of the outer wall by the river. In fact, it looked as though the outer wall and the wall of the keep were one and the same at that point.

"The river acts as a ready-made moat," Finn observed.

"On one side at least," said Thomas. "They dug the moat around the other three sides."

The pair continued in silence for a while. They were quite close to the castle when, all of a sudden, Thomas stopped abruptly, frowning.

"That is strange," he said. "The drawbridge is up."

EXCERPT FROM *WARRIOR HEROES*
BY FINN BLADE

DEFENDING A CASTLE

Castles are built to be easy to defend and very difficult to attack. The first line of defense is usually the castle moat--a huge, deep ditch surrounding the whole castle, filled either with water or sharp wooden pikes. To get across the moat, the attackers need to find a way of laying bridges across it. Of course, while they are doing this, they become easy targets for archers to pick off from the castle wall. Moats also make it difficult for attacking armies to dig tunnels under the castle to undermine, or weaken, it.

The next line of defense is the castle's outer wall and gatehouse. The outer wall is usually topped with battlements--huge stone blocks that protect the archers and allow them to shoot through gaps at the poorly protected attackers. Should enemy soldiers get as far as the outer wall and try to climb it, archers can rain arrows down on them from overhead. If that isn't effective enough, they will sometimes pour boiling water over enemy heads.

Finally, if somehow the enemy does get through or across the outer wall, everyone can retreat back to the main castle building--the keep --which is the strongest structure in the whole complex. The keep is almost impossible to break into.

CHAPTER 3

Arthur stood at the back of a desperate mob that was shouting across the moat to the soldiers in the castle.

Where is Finn? he thought, scanning the fields around the castle for any sign of his brother. *If he doesn't get here soon, we'll have no chance!* He breathed a huge sigh of relief when he caught sight of Finn approaching, and rushed over to meet him.

"Glad you could make it," he said to Finn. "They won't let anyone else in, and they've pulled the drawbridge up."

Thomas frowned. "That is not Sir William's way," he said. "He is a kind lord. And if they are not admitted to the castle, all these people will be killed."

Finn made introductions. "This is Thomas Shipton. We helped each other out of trouble. Thomas, this is my older brother, Arthur."

"Your brother did all the helping, friend," said Thomas ruefully. "He saved my life. It appears I may be able to return the favor sooner than I had thought. They will not keep me out of the castle." With that, he began to make his way through the crowd of people. Arthur and Finn followed behind.

When they reached the edge of the moat, Thomas turned to the furious group of men and women. They were hurling a mixture of curses, insults, and desperate pleas up at the guards on the castle walls and the large gatehouse at the castle entrance. A tall, blonde-haired young man appeared and stared down at the group with a sneer. The group instantly fell quiet.

"Keep running!" he shouted down to the crowd. "If you stay here any longer, you will be killed by John's men. That's if I don't give the order to kill you first!"

Thomas's face darkened. "Ralph," he spat.

"Not a friend of yours, then?" Finn asked.

"An arrogant bully. And he is trying to court the woman I love."

"Where is Sir William?" someone called, and

the shouting began again.

"Friends!" Thomas shouted above the din. "Friends, quiet. Let me speak with the guards. They know me."

Ralph caught sight of Thomas, and his sneer broadened into a malevolent grin.

"The castle is ready, Thomas," he shouted. "We prepare to defend against John the Withered. Have you heard? We will–" A shout from somewhere beyond the wall caused him to stop abruptly, and he turned toward the caller.

Moments later he turned back, his face scarlet. "Sir William instructs me to open the gates," he called out stiffly. "You may enter."

The crowd jeered and jostled as the drawbridge began its creaking descent over the moat. As soon as it reached the ground, the fearful mob stampeded over it and through the gatehouse, with Thomas, Finn, and Arthur at the rear. The boys crossed the threshold and stared up at the dark, looming walls of Wroxley Castle as the gates thudded shut behind them.

"This feels like a prison compound," Arthur whispered.

"Yeah," Finn agreed. "This kind of courtyard inside the outer wall is called a bailey, but prison compound sounds about right."

The new arrivals joined a throng of other nervous-looking people in the compound, whispering to one another and glancing fearfully up at the outer wall. Soldiers stared back at them from the top of the wall on either side of the gatehouse. Through the crowd of people, Arthur spotted Adam talking intently to a woman.

He was about to go over and introduce Finn to the man who had rescued him earlier, when someone called down to them.

"Friends!" the voice boomed. Finn and Arthur recognized the voice as quickly as they recognized the man. Sir William stood at the top of the outer wall and addressed the group.

"Every one of you is welcome to take refuge here. As you all know, the army of John the Withered marches upon us. By nightfall, we will be under siege. We have had very little time to prepare our defenses, and this afternoon, we will need to accomplish much if we are to withstand the attack. I ask that every healthy man, woman, and child make themselves available to assist in the defense of this castle in any way that they are asked. Those of you who were able to bring food or livestock, please hand it over to my men to be added to our supplies. We do not know how long the siege may last, and we may need every scrap of food we can lay our hands on."

Sir William paused for a moment, his eyes sweeping the crowd. "Now hear this. The punishment for any man or woman found stealing food is death. The punishment for any man or woman found to be spying for John the Withered is death. The punishment for any man or woman who attacks another within these walls is death. If we stand together, we may prevail. If we falter, we will be cut down. And I need not tell you that John the Withered will not be merciful." There was complete silence.

"I must go now to finish our plans for the

defense. For now, take some rest as best you can. You will soon be called upon."

Sir William descended the stairs of the outer wall and strode through the crowd, which parted for him as the people called out their thanks before he disappeared into the castle.

Finn and Arthur looked at one another anxiously. "How are we ever going to get Eleanor out of this?" muttered Finn.

Thomas let out a sigh. "Eleanor," he murmured. The boys followed his gaze and saw that he was staring up at a blue ribbon fluttering out from a tiny window slit near the top of the keep.

"The woman you love?" Finn asked, trying to sound calm.

"That she is," said Thomas. "A fairer maiden never walked this Earth. The ribbon at the window is for me."

Arthur grinned and pretended to gag behind Thomas's back. "And she's in there, is she?" he asked.

"Aye. Sir William will keep her there until the siege is over. It is the safest place for her. Though you may be sure she will challenge her father on it. She never cared much for safety..." Thomas trailed off, gazing wistfully up at the window.

Without warning, the tall, blonde man from before barged into Thomas, sending him sprawling into the mud. He landed awkwardly, a look of agony on his face as his wounded ankle hit the ground.

Ralph stood over him. "Poor Thomas, are you hurt?" he mocked. "My apologies. I did not see you in my haste. My lady Eleanor signals to me by that ribbon that she desires my company."

Thomas leapt to his feet and lurched toward Ralph, one hand on the hilt of his sword. But Arthur grabbed his arm and held him back. "Remember what Sir William said the penalty was for attacking anyone," Finn advised as Arthur tightened his grip on Thomas's arm.

Furious, Thomas struggled for a moment but finally relented.

"The boy is right, Thomas. Listen to your new playmate," Ralph goaded in a child-like voice. "Now I must go. Eleanor awaits, and Sir William will be requiring my presence at the battle council."

Arthur snorted. "He didn't care much for your decision about keeping these people out, but, yes, I'm *sure* he needs your advice now."

Sir Ralph's eyes widened in outrage. "How dare you! I'll have you flogged, you insolent dog." He sprang forward and grabbed Arthur roughly by the throat. "What is your name?" he hissed.

Arthur struggled, coughing and choking. He pulled at Ralph's hands in a desperate bid to free himself.

A circle had gathered around Arthur and Sir Ralph, formed entirely of the people who had just arrived at the castle.

"The boy is right," someone called out. "You tried to turn us away, and Sir William showed us kindness. Leave the boy alone!"

Sir Ralph's face reddened again and he spun around to face this new tormenter, pulling Arthur with him. But before the situation could develop any further, a thick-set man stepped out of the crowd. Arthur realized it was Adam.

"Sir William is waiting for you, Sir," he said.

Sir Ralph, though furious, saw that this was his chance to leave before his embarrassment became any worse. Flashing a final, hard stare at Arthur, he released his grip and stalked away toward the castle with Adam.

Coughing, Arthur fell to the ground. Finn and Thomas hurried over to him and helped him up, then led him to the outer wall. They all sat down. Thomas drew a deep breath and said, "Now you, too, have saved my life, Arthur. I could have killed him. What in God's name possessed me? He is a knight, and I a squire."

"I can think of a few other words to describe him," said Arthur, still struggling to draw breath. "You shouldn't have said what you did. I thank you for it, but Sir Ralph isn't going to forget it. He is a cruel man and he hates to be challenged. We must all watch each other's backs."

Thomas rubbed his ankle. "By heaven, this has been a day to remember already, eh Finn? Both of us were nearly killed in the forest. I nearly attacked a knight moments after being warned that the penalty is death. And Arthur here has already made an enemy."

"Actually, I nearly died earlier, too," said Arthur, and he filled them in on his near-drowning, omitting the part about waking up from time travel at the bottom of a river.

"Strange," Thomas mused. "So this Adam saved your life? In my anger, I thought nothing of it at the time, but I have never seen him before. Now, here he is, running messages for Sir William."

Arthur shrugged. He couldn't help but notice the troops of pages, squires, maids-in-waiting, castle guards, and servants within the castle walls. "There must be lots of people here today who you don't know. What's it like normally?"

Thomas explained to Finn and Arthur that

he lived in Wroxley Castle as a squire to Sir William's brother, Sir Godfrey. Sir William's daughter Eleanor lived there also. She and Thomas had fallen in love, though he could not openly court her until he was knighted. But then, the cruel and malicious Ralph had arrived, knighted too young in Sir William's view. He had little choice but to take Ralph in, though. He was the son of a wealthy baron. The new arrival had made no secret of his admiration for Eleanor.

"So when will you be knighted?" Finn asked.

"I know not," Thomas sighed. "I am only seventeen years. Too young for knighthood under ordinary circumstances."

"And does Sir William know about you and Eleanor?" Arthur inquired, trying but failing to hide his smile.

"Faith, no!" said Thomas. "And he must not!"

A young boy approached them from among the crowd of people, and they all fell silent. "Master Thomas, Sir Godfrey summons you."

"Farewell, my friends," said Thomas, getting to his feet and hopping slightly on his bruised ankle. "I shall find you this evening. In the meantime, remember–keep away from Sir Ralph. John the Withered is not the only man you should fear."

CHAPTER 4

Arthur and Finn had spent the day helping the soldiers to prepare the defenses. Barrels of cold water, quivers full of arrows, large bows, spears, lances, and various other weapons were now stacked neatly along the outer wall behind the battlements in readiness for the inevitable attack.

Guards stood along the top of the outer wall,

with even more backing them up from the top of the castle.

Arthur stood on the outer wall, leaning against the battlements and gazing out across the fields. The setting sun smeared heavy clouds with pink and purple, rendering the whole scene beautiful and strangely calm. Yet the situation was neither. Just beyond the range of the castle archers, John the Withered's army had made their camp. All afternoon, his soldiers and their supplies had trickled out of the forest and onto the plain. They swarmed like ants around the castle until they had it surrounded on three sides, with the river containing the fortress from the east. Tents and flags had been erected, fires lit, and other more sinister preparations made.

Looking west, Arthur could see a row of huge wooden catapults lined up, ready for a full frontal assault on the gatehouse and outer wall. *Trebuchets, not catapults,* Finn would have reminded him.

An enormous tree had been felled and transported from the forest to sit behind the catapults. A small group of men hammered away at it, most likely to shape it into a battering ram.

To the north, a group of men appeared to be constructing some sort of wooden tower on wheels.

"A siege engine," said Finn, in a hushed tone, walking over to stand with Arthur. "They use them to wheel soldiers up to the castle wall so they don't have to climb. I can't believe this is happening. We're actually in a full-on, medieval castle siege. Nice helmet by the way."

Arthur put a hand up to straighten his oversized helmet. Both he and Finn had been given one in preparation for the battle. Arthur wasn't sure whether Finn sounded geekily excited or just plain scared. "Yeah," he said. "And we're going to be on the front line with the archers. Are you OK with that?" When Thomas had told the castle sergeant about Finn's prowess with a bow and arrow, the boys had swiftly been instructed to join the archers when the attack began.

"I'm trying not to think about it," said Finn. "But listen, how are we going to get to Eleanor? We've got to get inside the keep."

"And why is that?" came a deep voice. The two boys jumped in surprise and turned to see that Adam had appeared at their side.

"Oh!" Arthur smiled. "Hello, Adam. Hey, thanks so much for calling Ralph away before. That's the second time you've helped me today. I really owe you now. Had Sir William really summoned him?"

Adam shook his head. "No, but I did what I could. You have a hot head, my young friend. You should be careful around men like Sir Ralph."

"Well, thanks again. This is my brother, Finn, by the way. We were just wondering whether we could see inside the keep at some point."

Adam looked at Arthur strangely, but before he could speak, one of the guards on top of the gatehouse blew a horn, signaling that someone was approaching the castle.

A single horse and rider were racing toward

the castle from the direction of the trebuchets. A knight who bore some resemblance to Sir William dashed out from the keep and mounted the steps of the outer wall two at a time. The rider reined in his horse and slowed to a stop on the other side of the moat.

"I bring a message from John the Withered!" the man shouted. "Where is Sir William?"

The knight appeared at the top of the gatehouse. "I am Sir Godfrey, Sir William's brother. What is your message?"

The rider smiled. "John offers mercy to you and to all those who are within your walls."

"How noble of him," Sir Godfrey snorted. "I find it strange that he comes with an army to offer mercy. What are his terms?"

"You must surrender this castle by nightfall.

If you do this and throw yourself on his mercy, then all will be spared."

"*Never!*" Sir Godfrey roared. "This castle and these lands have belonged to our family since the time of King William. We will not surrender them! And we will not send these good people out to be butchered by your soldiers. John has never shown mercy before, and he will not now. Begone!"

"Very well, Sir Godfrey," said the man, with a knowing smile. "May your death be as honorable as your words, for John desires you to know that if you do not surrender by nightfall, you, your family, and all who have taken refuge with you will be slaughtered like pigs."

"John has no claim to this castle," cried Sir Godfrey. "He is but a thieving rogue who bullies the weak. Leave now, scoundrel, or I will have you killed!"

The man below drew his sword and held it in front of his face, point up. "On guard then, and adieu!" The rider wheeled his horse around and galloped away, waving his sword over his head. As he did, a slow, heavy drumbeat started up somewhere in the enemy ranks. It was picked up along the line, until it thundered across the fields toward the castle from all directions.

"It begins," said Adam, and he turned away.

"Archers, to the walls!" cried the sergeant over the din of the drums, and for a while, there was frenzied activity as men rushed up to join those already on the wall. Already in position, Finn and Arthur stayed where they were, while others ran to positions on the ground inside the wall and stood nervously next to supplies of water and piles of blankets. Fires were lit in stone-ringed pits. Thomas rushed past the boys with a breathless, "Good luck!"

Sir William emerged from the castle and mounted the steps to the outer wall. He walked along it, clapping each archer on the back and offering words of encouragement. When he got to Finn and Arthur, he greeted them warmly.

"It is not our custom to send boys into battle, but young Thomas informs me that you fought bravely earlier today. We will need all the bravery in all of our hearts before this night is over. Fight well, boys."

He moved on. Everyone seemed to feel bigger and stronger after a few words from Sir William, and the boys were no exception.

Abruptly, the drumbeat stopped. The shouting inside the castle subsided, and a tense hush fell over both camps. Somewhere a river bird screeched, oblivious to what was about to take place, as the army of John the Withered waited for the signal to attack.

Finn stared over at Arthur, eyes round, nostrils flared, every sinew in his body taut like the bowstring in his fingers.

Then, through the still evening air came a creak and a whir as the arm of one enemy trebuchet swung up and over. Something shot up from the catapult, sailing high through the air, and crossing the divide between attackers and defenders. Finn noted with a sick feeling in his stomach that whatever it was appeared to have arms and legs. It flew over the archers' heads and landed with a *whumpf* on the ground inside the wall. It was plain for all to see that the first missile from the attacking army had been a horribly misshapen corpse.

"Dogs!" bellowed Sir William. "You will pay!"

The enemy reply was a blast on a horn, followed by a whole chorus of creaks and whirs as each trebuchet released its load.

Round, black, smoking projectiles flew at the castle like burning crows. One landed with a splintering crash on the parapet between Arthur and Finn, and suddenly the wall between them was engulfed in fire.

"Tar pots!" shouted Finn. "They won't damage the wall but don't get the stuff on you!"

Arthur had no intention of getting anywhere near it. On the ground inside the wall, pools of fire marked the spots where the pots had landed. One poor soul was running around in bigger and bigger circles, wrapped from head to toe in flickering fire. Someone eventually managed to wrestle him to the ground with a blanket and extinguished the flames.

Someone brushed past Finn with another blanket and started to smother the fire on the wall. More tar pots flew in a regular, grinding bombardment, and more fire splattered around the castle. The firefighters worked at full strength.

"They're advancing!" someone shouted urgently.

As fire rained down from the sky amid shouts of fear, the attacking soldiers marched forward, and the booming drumbeat resumed.

"*Archers, make ready,*" called the sergeant in charge of the archery line. Finn and Arthur

followed the lead of those to either side of them. They drew their arrows back, angling their shots slightly upward.

"*Release!*" boomed the sergeant, and a swarm of arrows arched toward the attackers, raining down on helmets, raised shields, heads, and shoulders. Some men dropped to the ground.

Their comrades did not falter, and stepped across the bodies, marching relentlessly on.

"Cover!" called the sergeant, and the defenders all crouched down as a shower of enemy arrows hissed and whizzed over the battlements. A man to Arthur's left screamed in pain and toppled backward off the wall, spouting blood from an arrow wound to the neck.

"Archers, ready!" called the sergeant again, and a second volley of arrows flew at the attackers. More men fell, and more bodies were trampled underfoot as the army continued its advance. They were running now, getting closer and closer to the moat.

"Shoot at will!" roared the sergeant, and any appearance of order was lost. Under a hail of fire and arrows, Finn, Arthur, and the other

archers peered out from behind the cover of the battlements, lined up targets, and shot them down.

Within seconds, the advancing soldiers had reached the edge of the moat. Behind them, the attacking army's archers redoubled their assault until the castle defenders felt as though they were under a permanent dark cloud of arrows.

A second wave of soldiers arrived at the edge of the moat, carrying a makeshift wooden bridge. It was hoisted up on its end and made to topple forward across the water. As the attackers swarmed over the moat, most of the archers that were spread across the outer wall rushed over to join Finn and Arthur near the gatehouse. Boiling water was brought up the steps and distributed along this part of the wall. While the archers continued unleashing their deadly arrows down onto the attackers, the boiling water was poured down from the battlements scalding anyone who tried to place a ladder against the outer wall.

Finn was shaking with fear by this time. His arms were aching, and his fingers were so slippery with sweat he could barely grip his bowstring. Out of nowhere, a ladder appeared on the other side of the wall in front of his face. He shouted for help. A man ran to his side with a long wooden pole. He began to push the ladder away from the wall just as the first enemy head appeared at the battlements. Finn dropped his bow and grabbed the pole in a frantic bid to help the man heave the ladder away from the wall. The ladder slowly toppled backward, sending the men on it crashing to the ground or into the moat below. Finn looked across to find Arthur, but then something stung his arm. Surprised, he stumbled backward, losing his footing. With a cry for help, he tumbled off the wall, his helmet flying off as he fell. He landed on something soft, hit his unprotected head on something hard, then lost consciousness.

EXTRACT FROM *WARRIOR HEROES*
BY FINN BLADE

CASTLE SIEGES

The whole point about a knights's castle is that an enemy can never get inside. Castles are made of rock, built on top of steep mounds, surrounded by moats and outer walls, and full of nasty little surprises like the holes through which defenders can pour boiling oil or water on attackers. But if you like a challenge, here are some things people have come up with to help break down castle defenses.

BATTERING RAMS

These are huge tree trunks tipped with iron that are hung

horizontally from wooden frames.
Teams of soldiers swing the trunk
back, then crash it forward to
break against the castle door.

MISSILES

A range of huge catapults have
been designed to fire missiles at or
over castle walls from a distance.
The best of these catapults can
throw a heavy rock very accurately
more than 655 feet (200 meters). But
some people use the catapults to
throw more than just rocks:

- You can throw firepots onto the
  castle roof to start fires.
- Or you could throw dead animal
  corpses over the walls to spread
  disease.
- And if you really want to get

noticed, throw the heads of dead
enemy soldiers over the walls to
terrify the poor souls inside
the castle!

UNDERMINING

Undermining means digging huge
warrens of tunnels underneath the
castle. As the tunnels are dug,
they are propped up with wooden
struts, then the wood is set on
fire. When the struts burn away,
the tunnels, and sometimes the
castle walls, will collapse.

SIEGE ENGINES

If you can't get under the walls
or smash your way through them,
then there is only one other
approach--over the top. To do this,

you'll need to build a wooden tower
on wheels, roll it up to the castle
walls, and jump across.

SIT IT OUT

If all that sounds like too
much work, there is an easier way.
Surround the castle with your
army, and don't let any food or
supplies in. Then just sit back and
wait. Sooner or later, the people
inside are going to want some lunch
and they'll come out.

CHAPTER 5

The first thing Finn became aware of when he came to was the throbbing pain in his arm. He opened his eyes and tried to sit up. But, as the room began to spin, he quickly slumped back onto the straw he had been lying on.

"Steady there, Finn," said Thomas, placing a hand on Finn's chest.

Finn looked, blurry-eyed, over to where

Thomas and Arthur were sitting. Beside Thomas was the most beautiful girl Finn had ever seen. Her piercing blue eyes stared intently out from a fine-boned face, framed by long, black hair.

"Your wound is not serious, but you do need to rest," she said, kindly.

"And you need to get back to the keep, my lady," said Thomas sternly.

"I will not spend any longer locked away in a big, stone prison," she snapped. "The wounded need help. Everyone in here is risking their life to defend the castle, and I do not wish to be any different."

"This is Eleanor," said Arthur to Finn. "In case you hadn't guessed."

"Wh... What happened to me?" Finn asked, attempting once more to sit up, but instantly falling back down. "And what about the siege?"

Thomas explained that Finn had been struck in the arm by an arrow and fallen from the outer wall. He'd landed on a straw bale, that luckily had broken his fall, but then he hit his head on a cart wheel that knocked him out. His arm had been bandaged by Eleanor who had been tending to the sick with her maids-in-waiting.

"You nearly made it to the end of the battle," said Arthur. "The attack was over a few minutes after you fell. You've been out cold all night."

"It's not the end, though. John's army will come again soon enough," said Thomas, grimly.

Finn looked around him for the first time. He was lying in a small makeshift tent that appeared to be set up close to the outer wall.

Through the open side of the tent, he could see the aftermath of last night's carnage. The earth was scorched where the tar pots had done their damage. From beneath a lumpy mound that was covered in matting, several legs and arms protruded.

Following Finn's gaze, Eleanor quietly said, "Too many people died last night. And all because of the greed of John the Withered. That is why we must fight him to the end."

"*You* need not fight him, my lady," Thomas protested.

"Oh, forgive my mistake, Thomas. Perhaps you would prefer it if I did what was expected of me and simply married a knight?"

Thomas looked crestfallen. "I do not mean to tell you what you can and cannot do.

I just do not want you to be killed," he said, eyes downcast.

Eleanor softened. "Perhaps you could accompany me as I visit the other wounded men," she said, gently.

Thomas perked up instantly and stood up. "I will, my lady," he said, puffing out his chest slightly. He nodded to Finn and Arthur. "Farewell for now, friends."

"He's got it bad," Arthur chuckled as Thomas and Eleanor turned to leave. But before they could, their paths were blocked by Sir Ralph at the entrance to the tent.

"My lady," panted Sir Ralph, out of breath. "I have been looking everywhere for you. You really should not be out here with these..." he looked scornfully over at the boys. "It is too dangerous, and this is no place for a young lady. Come back to the keep. You will be safe there." He moved to take her by the arm.

"I will do no such thing," replied Eleanor, her eyes flashing dangerously as she stepped out of his reach. But Ralph ignored the signs.

"My lady, you know of my affections." He glanced at Thomas and smiled cruelly. "But I must insist now. Do as I say and get back to the keep." He reached out to take Eleanor's arm, but she snatched it away.

"Men are all fools, Sir Ralph, but you are more foolish than most. I am not your child to order around. Nor are these others," she went on, indicating the boys.

Sir Ralph's face began its familiar transition to crimson. "You dare to–"

"Enough!" someone barked behind Sir Ralph. "Stand aside!" shouted Sir William, as he strode into the tent.

"Sir William," Ralph spluttered. "I did not mean to—"

"I heard enough of what was said. My daughter is right. She is not yours to command. Now leave."

Fuming, Sir Ralph turned on his heel and stomped away.

"Father," Eleanor began.

"And Sir Ralph is also right, in part. It is not safe for you to be out here. John's army might attack again at any moment. You must return to the keep. Immediately."

"But I want to help!" Eleanor implored.

"Then help by protecting yourself," her father

replied curtly. "If I am worrying about you, then I am not defending this castle as well as I might. This is not the time for us to argue, Eleanor. Please, go back."

With a face like thunder, Eleanor did as her father had asked. Sir William turned to Thomas. "Word reaches me that you fought bravely last night. You have my thanks. We will need that strength again today." He paused. "Eleanor is very capable of a brave fight also, is she not?"

Thomas was taken aback. Sir William had never spoken of Eleanor to him before. He could only nod and try to keep his jaw from dropping.

"She will find that there are some battles in life she cannot win. Marriage, for example," Sir William went on gently. "I wish it were not so, but she will not choose the man she marries.

He will be chosen for her soon enough, and he will be a knight."

Thomas lowered his gaze to the ground, his shoulders sagging slightly.

"These boys," said Sir William, turning to look at Arthur and Finn. "They are your friends?"

"Yes, Sir."

"Then you seem to choose your friends wisely, lad. Word has reached me that they, too, fought bravely last night. We must keep our spirits up, Thomas, or we will not prevail. You fought well, and when this is over, I will honor you all. Now," he said, turning away, "I must find Sir Godfrey. Perhaps you will come with me, Thomas." Too surprised to respond, Thomas simply followed.

After they left the tent, Finn groaned and

rolled over on his straw bed, clutching at his bandaged arm. Arthur frowned as his brother grimaced in pain.

"Finn, seriously, are you OK?"

"Yeah, other than being shot in the arm, almost dying defending a castle against attack, and falling off a wall and getting knocked out, I'm just great!"

"Well, we're both still here," said Arthur, trying to sound positive. "That's the main thing, right?"

"Yes, but what are we going to do?" Finn groaned. "We need a plan to get Eleanor out. If Sir William was right about the spy, then whoever it is must be in here with us somewhere. How are we going to persuade Eleanor to leave with us? Then how are we going to get out?"

"Beats me," Arthur shook his head. "I think all

we can do at the moment is try to survive." Both boys fell quiet, thinking about all they had seen the previous night.

"That was worse than anything we've–"

Finn was interrupted by the sergeant's booming voice. *"Archers, to the walls. They come again!"*

"I'd better go," said Arthur wearily. "If you start to feel better, try to get inside the keep and see what you can find out. You were wounded in battle; surely they must trust you now."

"OK," said Finn. "And Arthur...be careful up there."

Arthur smiled nervously as he put on his helmet and walked out of the tent.

Finn listened to the sounds of imminent battle, his head swimming with a panic of thoughts racing in circles. *Get her out before the spy takes her.*

Try to stop the spy. How do we convince her to leave? How do we escape? He felt dizzy. Nothing was clear.

He let go of his thoughts and lay back, his hand over his eyes. Gradually, beneath the shouts of the soldiers up on the walls, Finn latched onto a different sound—a whispered conversation that seeped through the canvas of the tent.

"She walks freely around the castle and outside. Why wait until she is in the keep?"

"We cannot get her across the walls during the day. We have to do this at night."

Finn held his breath. *The spy!* He could not believe his luck. Carefully, he rolled off the straw, trying not to lean on his injured arm, and crawled to the side of the tent so that he could hear more clearly.

"And we must do it this very night. With every

day that passes, Sir William will grow more and more concerned for her safety."

"Agreed. You have the potion?"

"Of course I do."

"Good. Then we must give it to her this night, and she will sleep like the dead."

"But we have no way of entering her room."

"We will find a way. When the battle is raging, we will not be heard."

The whispering stopped. Alarmed, Finn knew he had to find out who they were without being seen. Putting his head to the ground, Finn very carefully lifted the side of the tent just enough to see.

Rushing away from the tent was an unmistakable figure–Adam!

CHAPTER 6

Finn stumbled out of the tent and looked around. Adam had disappeared and there was no sign of whoever he had been whispering with. An arrow hissed into the ground next to Finn, making him jump. Not hesitating, he set off for the keep at a sprint.

He reached the doors and began hammering on them as hard as he could. There was no answer. All around him he could hear the crunches, crashes, and cries of battle. *Of course they won't hear me,* he thought. *What do I do?*

He looked back at the outer wall and saw Thomas running along it, carrying a burning torch and heading for a cluster of men a short distance from the gatehouse.

Finn's only thought now was to reach someone who would listen to him about the danger Eleanor was in. He sprinted over to the steps of the outer wall and bounded up them, the pain in his arm forgotten as a familiar mixture of fright and adrenaline numbed his nerves.

But, as he reached the battlements, he saw why the men had clustered together. A short distance from the wall stood the wooden siege tower that he and Arthur had seen the soldiers constructing the previous afternoon. The top of the tower was a little higher than the outer wall and several men were crammed inside it, all protected by a thick wall of wood. Some burning arrows were lodged in the timbers, but none of the fire had taken hold so far.

Finn stood transfixed as chaos swirled around him. A section of the tower clattered down like a drawbridge to make a platform that linked the tower to the battlements. Instantly, a group of soldiers thundered across it, wielding swords, battle-axes, and maces. They swung left and right at the defenders and formed a line of defense that protected their siege engine. The fighting was even more savage than on the previous day. Countless numbers of men toppled off both sides of the wall.

Unarmed, Finn could do nothing but watch as the battle raged before him. More men had appeared on the platform of the siege engine and were preparing to leap over the battlements to join their comrades. Finn saw Thomas lean out from the battlements and lob something at the platform. A shout went up from the attackers as the platform went up in flames and they were beaten back. The first wave of soldiers to cross the wall were picked off one by one until none of the enemy remained inside the wall. Tar pots were handed around to the defenders, who flung them at the tower. With the insides of the tower exposed by the lowered platform, the whole structure soon became a roaring inferno.

Finn hunched down behind the battlements and made his way toward Thomas, who was being congratulated by a weary-looking Sir Godfrey.

But before Finn had time to speak, the sergeant roared, *"Battering ram! Archers, ready! All other men to the castle gates!"*

In seconds, the wall on either side of the gatehouse was lined with archers, while a crowd of others, including Thomas, sped down the steps and put their backs to the gates.

The great oak trunk that the boys had seen the previous day had been sharpened to a point by the enemy soldiers, and tipped with iron. It swung back and forth, booming as the attackers smashed away at the castle gates, which shook and wobbled and creaked alarmingly. A relentless shower of arrows came from the archers above, but the men at the battering ram were well protected by a wooden roof that had been erected on top of the ram.

The gates began to make splintering noises, and the sergeant rushed down the steps, grabbing archers and telling them to follow.

"Tar pots!" he bellowed. *"Burning arrows!"*

Moments later, he had three lines of men facing the gates.

"Open!" he cried, and instantly, the gates were unbolted and flung open.

"Shoot!" The first line of men released a volley of arrows into the faces of the nearest attackers.

"Pots!" The second line flung the tar pots straight at the battering ram and under its roof.

"Shoot!" The final line of men shot burning arrows out through the open gates.

"Close!" With the enemy in disarray, the gates

were slammed closed again. The archers that remained on the wall picked off soldiers on the ground who were darting out from under the blazing roof of the battering ram.

A horn blasted in the distance and a great shout went up among the defenders as the attacking army began to retreat back across the moat again.

Finn caught sight of Arthur among the massed defenders and rushed to his side.

"Another attack foiled!" cried Arthur, gleefully. "But what are you doing up here? Are you OK?"

"It's Eleanor!" Finn gasped, and he poured out the whole story. It was only as he finished that he noticed Adam standing behind Arthur, a murderous look on his face.

"Sir Ralph!" shouted Adam, not taking his

eyes off Finn and Arthur. "You must hear this. It concerns Eleanor."

"What?" Finn spluttered. "No, wait!"

"Silence, boy," said Sir Ralph, appearing behind Finn. "What did you wish to say, Adam?"

Arthur tried to interrupt. "He's going to kid—"

"I said *silence!*" Ralph thundered, striking Arthur savagely across the face with the back of his hand.

Arthur's helmet flew off as he stumbled backward, clutching his stinging face. The victorious cheering of the men died down as they noticed what was happening.

"I believe these boys are spies, Sir Ralph," said Adam calmly. "And I believe they plan to kidnap Lady Eleanor."

Outrage and glee jostled for position on Sir

Ralph's face.

"Can you prove it?" he asked.

"I think so," said Adam. "But we should get them off the wall in case they try to escape."

"Quite right," said Sir Ralph. "You men, take these boys down to the ground and keep a good grip on them." But before any of the men could respond, Adam stepped forward and grabbed Arthur, pushing him down the steps and following directly behind him. Sir Ralph followed quickly.

Thomas came running up toward the brothers. "What is happening?" he cried.

"We are about to find out whether your friends here have been entirely honest with us," Sir Ralph replied. "Adam, if you would like to fill this *young* squire in."

"You don't understand," wailed Finn. "It's Adam. He's going to—"

"Enough from you!" Ralph shouted.

"I thank you, sir," said Adam. He turned to Thomas. "I overheard these boys discussing a plot to kidnap Lady Eleanor and take her to John the Withered as a hostage. They mentioned a sleeping potion that would prevent the Lady from resisting."

"Search them," Ralph barked. Two men stepped forward quickly to run their hands over the boys' clothes.

"This is madness!" said Thomas, but the words were barely out of his mouth when his eyes widened in shock. The man searching Arthur pulled a small stone bottle from the boy's clothes.

"What?" Arthur exclaimed. He pointed at

Adam. "He must have put it there when he brought me down the steps!"

Sir William strode up to the group. "What is the meaning of all this?"

"This good man," said Sir Ralph, nodding to Adam, "informed me that he overheard these boys plotting to kidnap Eleanor as a hostage.

It is my belief that they are spies for John the Withered."

"Spies?" Sir William snorted. "But they are just boys–mere children. Friends of yours, Thomas, isn't that right?"

Thomas said nothing, but stared from Finn to Arthur and back again.

"Thomas?"

"I believed that they were friends," he said, uncertain. "Finn saved my life. But, in truth, I met them only yesterday."

"Thomas!" cried Finn. "You must know–"

"Silence!" snapped Sir William. "I can take no chances over a threat to my daughter. You will be imprisoned in the keep until I have time to investigate this matter further. Take them away."

"But you have to believe the threat is Adam,"

protested Finn. "Watch him!" Finn shouted as he and Arthur were hauled away, both struggling against the iron grips of their guards.

The brothers had wanted to see the inside of the keep, but not this way. As they entered it for the first time, they immediately longed to be outside again. They were marched through dark halls, gloomy passages, and down a narrow staircase into a damp, cold basement. A couple of torches gave off just enough light to see by. The boys were pushed into a small, windowless room. As the door slammed behind them, they were struck by the grim realization that they were now locked inside a medieval dungeon.

EXTRACT FROM *WARRIOR HEROES*
BY FINN BLADE

MEDIEVAL WEAPONS
ARMOR

If you are a knight with a bit of cash, you'll wear chain mail or heavy metal plates as armor or both. This is good for stopping arrows and blades. Not so good for getting around quickly, or getting out of a moat if you fall in. On the other hand, if you're an ordinary soldier, you'll probably just wear some heavy leather clothes to try to keep the swords at bay.

Of course, you'll have the usual warrior's kit: ax, sword, knife, bow and arrow, spear, and shield. Depending on your combat style, you may have heavier weapons, too.

MACE

A mace is a very heavy object,
often spiked, attached to a handle.
The heavy part could be made of
metal or stone, and the handle
from wood or sometimes metal. It's
like a sledgehammer, which is quite
good if you're attacking someone
with heavy armor. With a mace, you
don't have to get through the armor
to hurt your opponent. You just
bash them over the head.

FLAIL

A particularly effective variation
on the mace is the flail, which is
a heavy metal ball with spikes all
over it, attached to a stick by a
length of chain. You can do some
serious damage with this weapon.

HALBERD

Think of a spear (for stabbing not throwing). Then add an ax blade on one side of the shaft near the spear point. Then add a nasty metal hook on the other side of the shaft. You can use this part to stab like a spear, swing like an ax, or pull someone off balance (or off their horse) without getting too close.

CHAPTER 7

Time seemed to change its meaning that day. Locked underground with no natural light, and left to stew in their fears of what might follow, the boys began to lose hope.

"They wouldn't torture a pair of kids," said Arthur. "Would they?"

Finn nodded slowly, sick with dread. "Sir William thinks we're spies, and this siege could go on for months. He'll do anything to defend the castle. I don't think they had child protection laws in medieval England."

Strange grunts, scrapes, and oaths echoed down the stone corridor. Both boys shifted uncomfortably on the hard, cold floor.

Finn remembered the Professor talking about castles and dungeons. He knew that, in medieval times, most castles didn't have real prisons or dungeons. Imprisonment wasn't a common punishment. Execution was far more likely.

"Hmm, if they really want to torment someone, they might use an oubliette," Finn mused.

"A what?" said Arthur.

"Nothing," said Finn, quickly. He hadn't intended to mention the oubliette out loud.

It didn't exist in all castles. It was used for the most horrible-sounding punishment he had heard of. The oubliette was a deep shaft in the ground with a lid on the top. The shaft was often so narrow that there was only room to stand and breathe. You couldn't sit, lie down, or even turn around. It was literally a manhole. If they really wanted someone to suffer, they would lower the poor wretch into the oubliette, stick the lid on, leave them in total darkness, and forget about them. In fact, the word oubliette came from the French "to forget." Finn shivered at the thought of it.

"Come on," Arthur urged. "There must be some way out of this."

"We're locked in a dungeon in a castle, Arthur. I don't think there is a way out this time."

"Well, think of something," snapped Arthur. "You always think of something."

"Really? What do you think our chances are?" Finn asked, sarcastically. "Let's see. We'll have to find Eleanor and convince her that she has to come with us, even though her dad thinks we're here to kidnap her. Then we'll have to find a way out of the castle in the middle of a siege. And, if by some miracle we manage all of that, we'll have to get past an army that has the castle completely surrounded. So, no, Arthur, I don't think I'm going to *think of something* this time!"

Finn stared miserably through a grate in the door. A shadowy wall of damp stone stared back at him in the faint torchlight.

"Not that it matters," he sighed. "We won't even get as far as that wall."

"Finn!" Arthur shouted, getting to his feet. "Get a grip. If we can't break out, then we'll have to think our way–"

The words died in his throat as the sound of boots approaching rang along the passage. Within seconds, Sir Ralph appeared at the bars of the door's window. He peered in at them with a sneer. Neither of the boys could meet his stare.

"I came to see how the boy spies are liking their new home," he mocked. "I told you I would make you pay," he went on, glancing at Arthur. "But I must confess, I did not see things shaping up this nicely. You may remember that Sir William's punishment for spies is death, yes?"

Finn winced at this, but Arthur looked up.

"You know it wasn't us!" he shouted, fists clenched in fury. "You were there! Why was

Adam so keen to be the one who pushed me down the steps? He planted that bottle on me."

"Really?" Sir Ralph replied, with an air of boredom. "Perhaps. Still, nobody else saw anything wrong, did they?"

"How can you be so stupid?" Finn blurted, scrambling to his feet to stand beside his brother. "Can't you see? If Adam is the spy, then Sir William is not safe and neither is Eleanor. The castle will fall, and you could have prevented it."

"Really?" Sir Ralph repeated in the same casual way.

Suddenly Finn realized what was happening. The idea made him feel sick. Ralph did know that Adam was the spy, and he didn't care. He wanted Adam to carry on. He wanted the castle to fall.

"You... you *do* know, don't you?"

"The castle will fall, you are right," replied Ralph, ignoring Finn's comment. "But Eleanor will be quite safe. I will see to that."

"How can you think that she will even look at you when she finds out what you're doing?" Arthur spat.

"Ha!" Sir Ralph exclaimed. "The girl really won't have much choice in the matter by the time John the Withered has finished here."

The boys were too shocked to speak.

"You do look wretched in there, you know," he went on. "But here is something that will cheer you up. In a few minutes, you will have some company." His cruel laugh sent a chill through the boys. What could he mean?

"Well, I must tell you that I have enjoyed our

little discussion. I don't think we'll be seeing each other again." With that, Sir Ralph's face disappeared from the door's window.

Finn and Arthur sat in silence. There was nothing to say. Adam would kidnap Eleanor. Sir Ralph would weaken the defenses somehow. John the Withered would sack the castle, and Sir William and all the rest would probably be killed. For their own part, the boys knew that they would probably die even sooner at the hands of Sir William who had been fooled by Adam and Sir Ralph's trickery. This, of course, was the most dismal thought of all.

"I wonder what the Professor would have done...," mused Finn. But neither boy could think of an answer.

Some time later, the clatter of boots reached

the boys' ears. Sick with dread as they awaited their fate, they heard the footsteps stop outside their cell. The boys shrank to the back of the cell. Someone unlocked the door and wrenched it open.

"In there," a gruff voice barked, as someone was shoved through the door and sent sprawling to the floor.

"Thomas!" cried Finn, as he recognized his friend. "What's happening? We thought you were the executioner."

"I may as well have been," Thomas replied, getting back to his feet. "I cannot apologize enough that I did not believe you earlier. Adam and Sir Ralph are plotting together."

"We know," said Arthur. "He came and told us all about it, the smug fool. But how did you end up down here?"

"I heard them plotting to attack Sir William during battle. They were planning to make it look like an accident. When they saw that I had overheard them, they did the same thing to me as they had to you, only this time they planted a letter in my pocket–from one of John's knights," Thomas said. "I could see that Sir William had his doubts, but he can take no risks now. So here we are, back together again. Tell me, what did Ralph say to you?"

Arthur filled Thomas in, not noticing Finn's attempts to steer him away from the subject of Eleanor until it was too late. By the time Arthur had finished, Thomas was in a state of complete despair. Finn wished he could say something comforting, but it seemed there really was nothing to say. The three prisoners sank into a brooding silence again, each lost in his own dark and desperate thoughts.

CHAPTER 8

Hours passed before Finn, lost in unhappy thoughts, became aware of the sight of dark shadows leaping on the damp stone walls outside their cell.

"Arthur. Thomas," Finn whispered, frowning through the darkness. "Someone's coming."

Once again, they retreated to the back of the cell as a hooded figure appeared at the door.

All three boys held their breath, not daring to move. Whoever it was looked each way along the passage, then turned a key gently in the lock, allowing the heavy door to swing open. Finn thought he glimpsed a lock of long, black hair, and a faint spark of hope rose in his chest. The figure threw back the cloak's hood.

"Eleanor!" the three of them gasped at once.

"Quiet!" she hissed.

Elated, Thomas rushed forward and embraced her. It was only as she gently pushed him away that the boys could see her face clearly. Tear-stained, pale, and drawn, it was a picture of grief.

"Eleanor, my love," Thomas soothed, "What has happened?"

"Father lies dying in his bed," she sobbed. "They say he was struck by an ax during the fight."

Thomas paled. "No...And what of Sir Godfrey and the castle?"

"Sir Godfrey lives and the castle has not yet fallen," said Eleanor, her voice cracking. "But it will fall soon. My father sent me here to..." she broke off, her breath coming too fast, and held a hand to her chest for a moment.

"...he wanted me to release all of you because he knows now that Sir Ralph is the traitor, not you," she went on. "He wanted me to bring you to him. He would not say for what purpose, but he said that we must not be seen. He does not know how many men's minds may have been poisoned by Ralph's treachery."

Arthur and Finn looked at one another knowingly.

"He sees what's coming," said Arthur, quietly.

"We must go now," said Eleanor. "He has not long to live."

Thomas reached a comforting hand out to her, but she shook her head and turned. "You need to follow me now."

Eleanor led them out of the dungeon and along the stone passage, past similar rooms once full of food and other supplies but now almost empty. They climbed a flight of steps. As they emerged from the basement, they heard the dreaded drumbeat that had announced the first attack on the castle. Over the sound of the drums came another booming sound they all recognized—the battering ram.

"Father says the defenses will not hold much longer," said Eleanor. She hurried across an empty hall to a door set in a curved, stone wall.

"This must be one of the towers," Finn whispered to Arthur, as they began climbing an uncomfortably narrow spiral staircase. Through the narrow slits in the stone, they could see that it was dusk outside. Smoke and screams filled the air.

"Who goes there?" came a gruff voice. The boys froze.

"It is I and three friends," Eleanor replied. The boys could not see around the twisting stairway to see what was happening. But, in a moment, they heard a door opening and their party began to move again. They followed Eleanor past a guard who nodded to them, and on toward two more guards blocking the next door. The guards parted when they saw Eleanor approaching. They opened the door for the group to enter a dimly lit bedroom.

Propped up on a pile of cushions lay Sir William, bleeding heavily through the chain mail he was still wearing from battle. His eyes were glassy and his face a terrible shade of gray.

Eleanor ran to him and knelt at his side, sobbing.

"Did you find the boys, my child?" Sir William wheezed. "My eyes are failing me. Are they here?"

"We are here, Sir William," said Thomas hoarsely.

"Ah, Thomas, my boy. It was wrong of me to doubt you. My judgment was clouded with fear. Fear for the castle. Fear for Eleanor. Will you forgive a dying man?"

"There is nothing to forgive, Sir William," he

said quietly, as tears filled his eyes.

"And your two friends. They fought so bravely for us, and I branded them liars and spies. Boys, where are you?"

Finn and Arthur stepped forward, uncertain what they should do.

"They are here, Father," said Eleanor, gently.

"Good. Good. This battle is nearly over, and John will have his way in a few more hours. Sir Ralph has been plotting against us from the first and now I lie dying..." Sir William coughed horribly. A trickle of blood seeped from his lips. He lay silent.

"Father, no!" cried Eleanor, stroking his head. With what seemed like a huge effort, Sir William spoke again.

"The castle will fall; that is certain. I will

die; that is also certain; and, tragically, so will most of those who fought alongside us. I have failed to protect them, but there is one thing I can still protect. The most precious thing of all..." he said, as he squeezed Eleanor's hand. "You must live. You must escape."

"Father, no. How can I live and let you die?"

"You *must* live, Eleanor." Sir William insisted. "If I know that you will live, then my death may not have been entirely worthless. If you do not escape, then you will either die or be taken against your will by Ralph to live a life that feels like death. Make your escape, child—you and Thomas and these boys."

"Father, no, please," cried Eleanor in anguish.

"Eleanor, it is my dying wish. You may not argue with me on this. Godfrey knows."

"He will stay and fight to hold John back for as long as possible. But he will not confront Ralph until you are gone. You must escape. Live, grow, and one day you may find a way to reclaim this castle for your family. That is my wish, child." Again he broke off, coughing more blood onto his chin.

"Thomas, my boy. You will protect my daughter?"

"With my life, Sir William."

"Then there is one last act I must perform," said the knight, his voice barely more than a whisper now. "Somebody pass me my sword."

Arthur had seen Sir William's sword at his bedside the moment they entered the room. He reached for the sword, and laid it on the bed next to Sir William, then placed the

dying man's hand on its hilt.

"Thomas, I said to you yesterday that my daughter would one day soon marry a knight. So kneel."

Stunned, Thomas fell to his knees beside the bed.

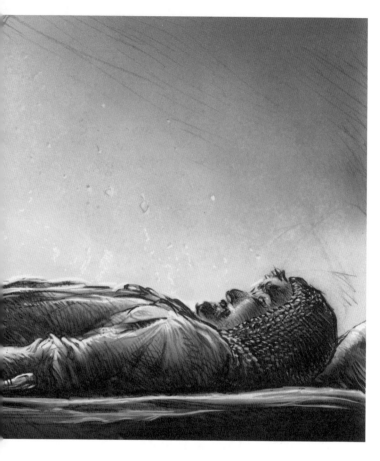

"Place your hands on mine, Thomas, on this sword."

Thomas did as he was told.

"If you wish to marry my daughter, then you have my blessing. Protect her as I have done. No, protect her better than I have done. Take her from here, and take your two friends also. They are too young to die in battle. Take this sword of mine and make good your escape. Now, arise, Sir Thomas Shipton."

Thomas stood, tears streaming down his cheeks. Eleanor laid her head on her father's chest and sobbed.

"Boys," Sir William whispered. "There are more weapons in the chest beside the bed. Take them." Gently, he lifted Eleanor's face in his hands and smiled.

"Now go," he whispered. "Before it is too late."

Unable to speak, Eleanor kissed his forehead and stood. Thomas placed an arm around her shoulders. Finn and Arthur each took an armful of weapons and followed them to the door.

"Goodbye, Father," Eleanor sobbed, turning back one last time.

"Goodbye, my love," he replied. "Goodbye, children. And good luck."

EXTRACT FROM *WARRIOR HEROES*
BY FINN BLADE

BECOMING A KNIGHT IN THREE SIMPLE STEPS

STEP 1: Try to make sure your dad is a knight, then get the lord of the local castle to take you on as a page at around eight years old. You'll be taught how to fight with wooden spears and swords, and how to ride a horse properly. Unfortunately, you'll also have regular, boring lessons in reading, writing, Latin, and possibly dancing and essential fighting techniques. Get really good at all this stuff.

STEP 2: When you're around sixteen, you should be made a squire. This is supposed to be a promotion from being a page. You will learn how to fight properly in heavy armor, use real weapons, and joust. But you'll also have to be a servant to a knight. This means serving him all his meals, cleaning up after him, carrying his things on the way to jousts, and possibly going with him to battles to look after the tent while he's out killing people.

STEP 3: When you're around twenty, you'll be knighted if people think you're ready or if they really need a few more knights for a battle that's coming up. Your lord will "dub" you a knight. Forget all this gentle tapping of swords on shoulders. In reality, part of the dubbing ceremony involved the squire getting punched and knocked over. This was supposed to remind him of what he was really there for.

Congratulations, you're now a knight! Now your lord can order you into battle whenever he feels like it.

CHAPTER 9

As the two guards outside the room closed the door behind them, Arthur turned to Eleanor.

"Can we speak in front of these guards?" Eleanor nodded, tears still streaming down her face.

Arthur went on. "We are so very sorry about your father, and I hate to do this so quickly, but we have to make a plan. How do we get out of the castle? We don't want Ralph to see us, and we can't be spotted by the attackers, either."

"Is there an escape tunnel?" Finn asked, hopefully.

Eleanor shook her head and took a deep breath. "If Father wants us to escape and survive, then we will need some rope. Can you both swim?"

The boys nodded.

"Good," she went on. "Father always said that the only way to escape Wroxley Castle in a siege would be along the river, downstream from the mill. The keep drops straight down to the bank there, and there is no outer wall."

Arthur shivered. He had nearly died in that river. It was strange to think that he only survived because Adam had been there and wanted someone to help get him into the castle.

"We'll need to get back to the cellars for rope," said Thomas.

"I will go alone," said Eleanor. Before Thomas could protest, she raised her hands. "I know, I know. You want to protect me. But think–if I am seen, nobody will question why I am there. However, if *you* are seen, we will be attacked. I am safer–we are *all* safer– if I go alone. Wait here. I will be gone just a few minutes."

"At least take a sword," said Arthur, handing one over. She nodded and fastened the sword belt around her waist. She touched Thomas's arm and stepped out of the hall onto the staircase.

Thomas immediately began pacing.

After a few silent minutes had passed, Thomas

muttered, "I should go after her."

"No," Finn said. "She's right. We all have a better chance if we stay here."

Thomas turned to the guards. "You are aware what is going on?" The two men nodded.

"Nobody other than Sir Godfrey is to enter Sir William's room. If you see Adam or Ralph..."

"We will kill them instantly," growled one of the guards.

Thomas nodded and began pacing again.

"Where do we go from the river?" asked Finn, at length. He was keen to keep Thomas talking.

"I do not know," Thomas replied. "If we can get past the enemy line, it will be dark. Eleanor and I know the land well. Even though all of John's men will be attacking Wroxley Castle, we will still have to be careful. But perhaps we might make our escape unnoticed. The hardest task will be getting into the river unseen, and swimming past the enemy."

Suddenly, the guard on the stairs barked, "*Who goes there!*" The door opened and Eleanor reappeared, carrying a length of rope and a few dark brown cloaks. Thomas rushed to her side.

"Put these on," she said, throwing the cloaks to the floor. "We will not be seen so easily."

Moments later, all four of them were cloaked, hooded, and armed with an assortment of daggers, swords, bows, and arrows.

Eleanor looked longingly at the door to her father's room, then turned away. "Follow me," she said.

She led them down the stairs a short way, then along an unfamiliar passage. It opened into an empty round room, like a landing between two more twisting flights of stairs.

"This is the place," she said. "From here, we can climb straight down to the river."

Thomas uncoiled the rope and tied one end to a thick pillar in the middle of the room.

Eleanor peered out through a small window. "Good," she said. "Complete darkness and no moon."

Thomas took the loose end of the rope and fed it steadily out through the window until the last section pulled tight against the pillar.

"I will go first, in case there are any surprises at the bottom," he said. "Eleanor, you follow, then Arthur. Finn, while each of us is climbing down, watch over us with your bow at the ready."

Arthur put a hand on Thomas's shoulder. "Wait, what happens when we get to the bottom or if we get separated?"

"At the bottom of the castle wall is a very thin ledge of earth before a steep bank. We should be able to wait there, then enter the river together. If we are separated, then we'll gather on the other side of the first bridge we come across. That bridge is nearly half a mile away, but the current is strong and it will not take long to reach."

"Can we find anything to float on?" asked Finn, nervously. "Perhaps we could try to break up one of these doors."

Eleanor shook her head. "There will be too much noise, and it will take too long," she said. "We must go now."

Thomas nodded to the boys, kissed Eleanor's hand, and climbed awkwardly through the small window. Finn poked his bow through and leaned out after him—an arrow notched and ready to shoot at the first sign of any danger. Hand over hand on the rope, Thomas lowered himself to the bottom, walking his feet down the side of the castle wall.

The attack seemed to have intensified around the walls near the gatehouse. But, while the fighting sounded more frantic than ever, the wall around the corner by the river appeared to be deserted.

"Your turn," said Finn, making way for Eleanor to climb through the window. "See you at the bottom."

Again, Finn acted as lookout, and again, there was no sign of any direct threat outside. But as Eleanor reached the ground, Finn and Arthur heard footsteps on the stairs inside the tower.

Finn ducked back inside, glancing at Arthur, his eyes wide in panic.

"Quick," Arthur whispered, "we'll go together. Out!"

Finn threw his bow over his head and scrambled out through the window, clutching at the rope as he lowered himself a few feet down the wall. Steadying himself and gripping the rope tightly, he looked up to see that Arthur had followed quickly behind him.

"Go!" Arthur instructed, as soon as he was out, and the two boys slipped and snatched their way down as quickly as they could.

They had not yet reached the ground when Finn heard a door opening, then a shout. Glancing down, he saw Thomas and Eleanor on the ground staring up at him.

It was still too far for Finn to jump safely. "Go now!" he shouted down to them as a shout of alarm came from the window above.

"They've seen us!" yelled Arthur, and Finn looked up again to see the outline of a head sticking out from the window.

"I'll kill you, you little rats!" Finn recognized Ralph's furious voice. He slid down painfully as fast as he dared. The rope burned his hands.

"He'll cut the rope," Arthur shouted. "We have to jump!" Finn knew he was right. He kicked out from the wall and let go of the rope, praying that he would clear the riverbank and land in

the water. Time slowed and the fall seemed to last forever. Finally, a wall of freezing water smacked Finn in the back. He gasped as the water took hold of his body and dragged him away.

He heard a splash and twisted around. At first, he could see nothing but swirling water. Then Arthur's head bobbed up, coughing and cursing. Finn lay on his back letting the current take him.

The cries and screams of battle grew louder as the river took him past the entrance to the moat that ran around to the gatehouse. He could see nothing of the fighting. The shadowy outline of the castle began to recede and, moments later, was swallowed up by the night.

He drew a breath in, thinking he would call out to find out whether Eleanor and Thomas were ahead of him. He thought better of it when he remembered they may not yet be clear of the attacking army. Turning onto his front, Finn swam along with the freezing current until he began to make out the dark shape of a small stone bridge ahead. He tried to kick closer to the bank, but the river was too strong. His wounded arm, which he had barely noticed for the past day, now throbbed painfully as he passed under the arch of the bridge.

The rushing roar of the river intensified up ahead, but Finn could hear Eleanor's voice calling to him.

"Finn, stand up!"

He felt something scrape against his knee. He thrust his feet downward to find he was sliding across shallow water over slippery pebbles and rocks. He stood up, staggering as the river tried to pull him forward, and turned in time to see Arthur heading straight for him. The boys gripped each other by the hand and slipped and wobbled their way to the riverbank.

Finally, they slumped onto dry land, exhausted and freezing, but alive–and reunited with Eleanor and Thomas.

CHAPTER 10

It was long past midnight by the time the shivering, dejected group dragged the door of a shepherd's hut closed behind them and sank to the floor.

"F-f-f-ire," Thomas stuttered through his chattering teeth.

Arthur found a small pile of dry wood and set to work building a fire in a pit in the center of the hut. Eleanor found some sheepskins, and everyone huddled close around the fire pit. Steam from their wet clothes mixed with the wood smoke. The fire grew steadily hotter, and they gradually began to feel a little better.

They stared into the flames, each of them lost in thoughts about all they had been through.

"What next?" Arthur wondered out loud.

"What next?" Eleanor repeated. "Well, if we are going to live, then we had better eat." She pulled some cheese and salted pork from a bag she had carried under her cloak. "It is a little bit wet, of course, so if you would prefer to wait..." She broke off and handed the food around. "You all look hungry."

They tore into the food, devouring it in seconds.

And, for a while, they forgot their sorrows. They were not out of danger, but they had survived, and it felt good. Arthur made everyone laugh with an impression of Ralph at the window. Eleanor teased Thomas about being a great knight, and Finn teased both of them about getting married.

"Well, you two must join us at the wedding," Eleanor laughed. "We could not have done this without your help." Finn looked sadly at Arthur.

"Eleanor is right," said Thomas. "You have both done so much. You have saved both of our lives and have proved yourselves to be the truest of friends—all in a mere two days."

A sudden knock at the door silenced the room, and for a moment, nobody dared move. Finally, Thomas slowly got to his feet, drawing his sword. With a backward glance at the rest of the group, he hauled the door open. An old man stood in the doorway, his palms facing forward.

"We mean no harm," said the man.

"Are you with John the Withered?" Thomas demanded, pointing his sword directly at him. "How many of you are there? Why are you here?"

"I am a shepherd, and this is my hut," the man replied. "John's men burned our village to the ground. Only a few of us have survived. May we enter?" The man stepped aside to reveal a group of five men and women, and two small children, all looking frightened.

"I recognize this man, Thomas," said Eleanor, getting to her feet. "He worked on my father's land. Let them in."

Seeing no threat, Thomas stood aside and

ushered the group into the hut.

Out of respect for her position, none of the new arrivals looked Eleanor in the eye. "You are kind, my lady," said the old man.

"Just as my father was," Eleanor replied, her eyes misting over. "Wroxley Castle will fall soon. We cannot stay here long."

"I thought as much," said the old man. "Where will you go?"

Thomas said, "My father lives some fifty miles from here, and he will give us all safe refuge. It will be a dangerous journey, but far less dangerous than staying here. John's men will put all their energy into the attack on the castle for a short while longer, but then some of them will disband. I would not want to be discovered by those devils after they've sacked a castle."

"This hut may well have saved our lives, old man," Thomas continued. "If you wish to accompany us to my father's house, then we would be honored."

"You too are kind, sir," said the man. "We will certainly come with you. May I ask your name?"

Arthur quickly broke in. "This," he said proudly, "is Sir Thomas Shipton."

* * *

Finn woke with a start and sat up. His arm throbbed from the arrow wound, his head throbbed from the freezing river, and his back ached from sleeping on a hard floor. Not quite knowing why, but following instinct, he crept to the door and slipped out of the hut. He was surprised to find Arthur already there.

Away to the east, the first rays of the morning sun were lancing across the sky. They saw now that the old man's hut sat at the top of a long ridge. As they looked down into a valley, they saw a sea of morning mist floating below them.

Arthur looked at Finn and smiled. The mist began to swirl and tumble up the side of the valley, like an avalanche in reverse.

"Eleanor's safe now," said Finn.

"We're going home!" Arthur shouted triumphantly as the mist began to surround them, growing thicker and thicker until they could not see one another. Slowly, the hut, the valley, the castle, and their friends vanished completely.

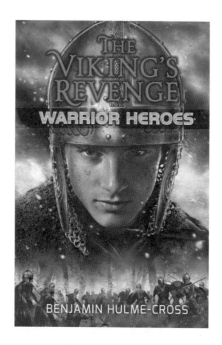

WARRIOR HEROES
The Viking's Revenge

Benjamin Hulme-Cross

Trapped in their great-grandfather's museum by a
group of terrifying ghosts, Arthur and Finn must
travel back in time to help restore the famous
Viking sword, Blood Hunter, to its rightful owner
and escape the clutches of a fearsome Viking tribe.

Extract from
WARRIOR HEROES
The Viking's Revenge

Arthur shivered, wondering where the cruel screeching was coming from. His bones ached from the cold. His face was wet and his nostrils were full of the smells of leaves and mud. He didn't want to wake up. But of course, as soon as you think that, you always do.

Find Blood Hunter!

He rolled over onto his back and opened his eyes, slowly letting in the thin dawn light. A spider crawled out of his hair and down his cheek. The screeching of birds continued.

"Finn!" he croaked. Looking around, he saw nothing but trees in all directions. *I must be in a forest somewhere,* he thought. He scanned the trees for any sign of his younger brother. Nothing.

Arthur had no idea where he was. He concentrated hard. An image of an old man looking down at him very seriously flashed before his eyes. His name danced around the edges of Arthur's memory.

"Good luck," he said "and be brave." Then another man stepped into view, huge and bearded, wearing a helmet. Arthur's memories rushed into focus: Professor Blade...the Hall of Heroes...the Viking...*Find Blood Hunter!*